THE WOMAN ACROSS TH

(A new story in the series 'A Twist in the Tale')

Chapter 1

She harboured dark thoughts as she stared out
from her rain-streaked front window and gazed
at nothing in particular other than the storm-
blackened clouds. The fact was, there was
nothing in particular that drew her attention. The
black bins had been emptied yesterday morning
with the usual banging and clanging that
accompanied it although the elderly gentleman
living next door hadn't yet taken his in. It stood
on the pavement at an angle and when the street
grew darker during today's winter afternoon, it

1

would present a hazard to pedestrians and to buggies pushed by mothers or fathers out jogging. Parents really should instruct their children not to scoot their boards along pedestrian pathways either. There was a playground within ten minutes walking distance. Yet another accident waiting to happen. It better not happen to her or she'd exchange words and unpleasant words at that!

*

The evening's light was fast disappearing and the black bin still hadn't been moved. What was wrong with the man?

She had a sudden thought and it sent a shiver down her spine.

2

Was there something wrong with him?

Mabel Apthorpe believed she was slightly older and, therefore, wiser than her neighbour-across-the road - not that you would think so if you stood them side by side, she thought. *That* neighbour could do so such more to improve her appearance and her attitude which was far from welcoming.

Apart from a curt 'good morning' or a grudging 'good evening' few words were ever exchanged between them.

Mabel knew very little about her immediate neighbour – the one next door to her. Not that she was unfriendly or distant towards him or he towards her so far as she could tell.

3

His surname was '*Woodman*' and she was aware
that his first name began with the letter 'G'.
These facts she knew only because the village
postie had once wrongly pushed a letter through
her letterbox addressed to him. That might have
been three years ago or maybe four. Could it be
five? Time either flies by or it lasts through
endlessly dull days and sleepless nights.

She peeped surreptitiously from behind the
front-room curtains and was surprised to see his
black bin *still* on the pavement beside his fence.
One thing she did know about 'G Woodman'
was that he was punctilious. He put out his bin at
exactly the same time each Monday morning,
Bank Holidays excepted, and he wheeled it back
down his garden path within minutes of it having

been emptied into the Council's refuse collection lorry.

Strange that. Perhaps he wasn't well.

Mabel considered knocking on his door but decided against it. You never knew who might be peeping through their curtains although she had a pretty good idea who it would most *likely* be ... that woman over the road! The one always standing in the shadows of her bay window where she thought herself hidden from the prying eyes of passers-by.

Best not to knock on his door then. Better to wheel the bin through his gate and leave it by the back door. That would be quite a neighbourly thing to do. Perhaps it was better to leave it until the morning as it was growing dark and one could never be sure who might be lurking in the shadows. On the other hand, if she did it now, in the mounting darkness, she could take a sneaky look through his kitchen window and see how tidy he kept it. In her limited experience of such matters, she was quite sure that men considered washing up and polishing the taps a low priority.

Chapter 2

'There's Mabel Apthorpe cosying up to her neighbour', observed the woman who lived opposite.

Maybe she was looking for a man, Heaven

forbid! Mabel had never married, apparently, according to Mary, the chatterbox who worked in the village's general store. From where did all the gossip she acquired emanate? Never mind whether any of it was true or not, it kindled her imagination. Little else did these days.

Why would her neighbour be seeking a man in her life anyway if she'd chosen not to marry? Or had nobody chosen to marry *her*? Was there something odd about her? Mind, there hadn't been a man in her *own* life for well-nigh forty years. The rotten sod had upped and left her for a woman with dyed hair! Ten years younger than him, too. What on earth had she seen in that idle layabout of a man? It certainly wouldn't have been his looks. A respectable lady would be repelled by the sight and smell of his unshaven face, unkempt appearance and sweaty odour.

She pondered crossing the road and wheeling the black bin along the path that led to his front door.

Another five minutes and I'd have done that, she thought. Anyway, Mabel had done it now and the pavement was free of an obstruction. That was the main thing.

*

Mabel thought about calling out through the letterbox but what would she say?

'Everything all right, Mister Woodman? I've brought in your dustbin.'

8

Perhaps she should leave a note and simply sign it '*Mabel from next door*' so that he knew exactly which neighbour had been thoughtful enough to step forward.

She'd write no more than that in case he misinterpreted it and read more into the note than intended.

Chapter 3

The following morning, the woman across the road noticed that the black bin was still standing beside Mr Woodman's front door exactly where Mabel had left it the night before.

That couldn't be right. Surely he would have wheeled it down the passage and left it by his kitchen window?

She wondered...should she pop over and knock on his door?

Probably not wise. Mabel was sure to be watching from behind her half-opened curtains and might misinterpret the reason behind her visit and consider her a man-hunter! It didn't bear thinking. She was simply a good neighbour concerned for the welfare of those living close by.

*

Whilst she was considering her safest course of

action, a car pulled up outside Mister Woodman's house.

Mabel spotted it, too, and immediately summed up its owner. She had a knack for such things.

The car was an old blue Ford Focus. She called it a Ford Focus because she could recognise the logo below the boot lid. It read *'Ford'* and the only Ford she knew of was called Focus. No doubt there were other models but she didn't drive, never intended to, never asked for lifts and considered the bus perfectly adequate, inexpensive (she had a bus pass!) and environmentally friendly. Friendlier than some people, in fact. People like Mrs Wilson who never passed the time of day when she was out with her horrible little dog. What was the point of smiling at her when a stony-faced look and a yapping dachshund was her reward?

*

A man got out of the old blue Ford Focus and looked about him. Either he was confirming he had the correct address or checking that nobody was watching him.

He saw no curtains twitching, no dog-walkers and no sign of activity from the growing tribe of keep-fit joggers and walkers that puffed their way around the village.

The man rang the front door bell. After fifteen

seconds he rang it again. The door remained shut.

*

The woman living opposite sighed with relief. Mr Woodman's visitor would not be parking his car for heaven knows how long, blocking her view through the curtains into the room where Mr Woodman seemed to spend most of his day watching television. There were, quite simply, too many cars parked outside houses on her pretty street. Some owners actually parked them half on the pavement! She hoped somebody would come along one night and snap off their wing mirrors. One of those juvenile delinquents that lived on the nearby crowded estate. Their

13

parents never knew where they were or what they were up to. Probably didn't care either so long as nobody raised a complaint or called a policeman.

*

There being no reply, the man looked casually to his left and to his right and then withdrew a key from a trouser pocket.

Mabel Apthorpe opened her curtains a fraction more and from the corner of one eye watched as he inserted the key into the door and then pushed it open. She tut-tuttted to herself. He hadn't allowed sufficient time for her to gain even a glimpse of her neighbour's wallpaper. The door hadn't been opened sufficiently wide. She normally kept a pair of old binoculars handy on a dresser close by but had left them in the kitchen so that she could keep a look out for the ginger cat down the road. It made a point of creeping into her back garden and scaring away the little birds that came for their daily breakfast of bread and seeds. They were her friends.

Chapter 4

A few minutes later the man left by the side door and tossed something into the empty black dustbin.

Mabel and the woman from across the road, who was still testing her new NHS hearing-aid, thought they heard a dull thump before the lid clattered shut and the man returned to his Ford Focus. They watched him swing his car around and head back along the road from wherever he had come.

"Really!" Mabel thought. He hadn't even checked for cyclists or pedestrians.

"Pity there isn't a speed camera to nab him," the woman across the road grumbled as he roared away.

*

Dixon Clarke drove his blue Ford Focus to the closest County Police Station and waited by the reception counter as an inebriated young woman explained why she had removed her clothing in a local park and begun jogging around its perimeter.

"Yes, miss, you do have the right to freedom of expression but others have an equal right to be protected from harassment, alarm and distress...and we received a complaint from a mother out with her two children."

"Which of her three rights was the mother complaining about?" the young woman asked.

While this was being discussed, a young police officer stepped into the reception area and asked how he might help.

"My uncle has been murdered," Dixon said with

forced nonchalance. "His name is Geoffrey Woodman."

"I see. Well, sir, could we start with your name, please?"

"Dixon Clarke."

"Why do you say he's been murdered? And how do you know?"

"I called at his house no more than thirty minutes ago. He didn't answer the door bell so I let myself in."

"You had a key?"

"Well, yes. He gave keys to family members in case there was an emergency."

"Did you call for an ambulance?"

"It was too late for that."

"How can you be sure that he was dead?"

Dixon sighed.

"His throat had been cut. His head was almost hanging off his shoulders...and he wasn't breathing … and his tongue was missing."

"Missing? Are you sure?"

Dixon eyed the young police officer for several seconds.

"Open your mouth."

"What?"

19

"Just open your mouth. Pretend I'm your dentist."

The man tentatively did so.

"There it is! I can see it. Your tongue."

The policeman frowned.

"So...?" he asked.

"So, I know what a tongue looks like, okay? When I saw blood spread across my uncle's face I prised open his mouth. His tongue was missing."

"I see," the young officer said. "One moment, if you please ... I think I'm about to be sick."

20

Chapter 5

A couple of police officers were knocking on doors in Sycamore Road asking occupants whether they had noticed any unusual or suspicious activity at Mister Woodman's home recently. Two of them had.

Mabel Apthorpe lived next door to Geoffrey Woodthorpe and she spoke of her concern over his black bin being left on the pavement and posing a hazard to young mothers with pushchairs.

The woman across the road had spotted the driver of a blue Ford Focus entering and, later, leaving the house. She had been curious but noticed nothing that she would call 'suspicious'.

When asked if she had anything further to add, she had replied,

"It would be helpful if they had a weekly rather than a fortnightly black-bin collection."

*

Mabel waited until it had grown dark before venturing out.

A nearby lamppost gave out a dull glow which did little to illuminate the cracked paving slab outside her house. If she hadn't been wearing sensible shoes and her new prescription spectacles from Specsavers she might have tripped on it a few nights ago when out peering through the part-opened curtains of neighbouring houses.

*

The woman across the road hastily closed the gap in her own curtains before turning the lights back on. She had nothing to hide but that didn't mean she wanted anyone to *see* what she wasn't hiding!

As she took a final glance through her window, she spotted Mabel's shadowy figure half-stumble on the pavement before raising the lid of her neighbour's black bin.

The council should do something about that broken pavement before there was a nasty accident.

*

Mabel was often curious. She wasn't nosey but she didn't like what she referred to as '*mysteries*'. One such '*mystery*' was what the man in the blue Ford Focus had put into the black bin before he had driven away, somewhat recklessly, the other night.

Glancing right, left and over her shoulder, she considered herself unseen and undetected.

It would be the best part of a fortnight before the refuse collectors returned to this neck of the woods to empty black bins. Before that she would have to tolerate the din that accompanied the emptying of both blue and green bins! Double the noise. Double the inconvenience to foot travellers such as herself.

Although convinced nobody could see her in the darkened street, Mabel, nevertheless, continued peering into the gloom around her searching for prying eyes. Some folk in the neighbourhood switched their inquisitiveness from mere curiosity to plain *nosiness* when it suited them!

The black bin was still by the back door, a house number crudely hand-painted on the front in white numerals. She raised its lid tentatively as though she thought some wild creature might leap out and bite her nose.

The weak light from the torch she carried needed

fresh batteries but its glow should be sufficient for no more than a quick glance of the bin's interior. Mabel remembered that she was actually carrying two fresh batteries in one of her dress pockets but sorting out which end up to insert them in *daylight* was problem enough let alone in darkness.

Chapter 6

A dog barked. Its lead was stretched tight as it dragged Mr Herman in the direction of the stifled scream.

Mabel's neighbour from across the road just beat Mabel in being first to peer out from behind her curtains but within a matter of seconds curtains were twitching in other windows, too.

The dog stopped when it reached the house of Mr Woodman and pawed at the gate. The gate creaked open on its unoiled hinges, the sound sending an unexpected chill down Mr Herman's spine. It reminded him of ghost stories he had read when much younger. This, in turn, made him feel ridiculous. He was a grown man. A bit on the short side, perhaps, at five feet four, but fully developed, nevertheless!

"Shush, Tyson!"

Mr Herman pulled his dog closer, advanced several feet and then halted abruptly.

A woman was on her knees beside a black dustbin. She was whimpering softly to herself as she rocked gently back and forth. He winced as he bent his back and lowered himself to her level. Damn! An entirely unrelated thought struck him. He'd forgotten to take his evening dose of blood pressure medication.

There was a small, black plastic bag just beyond the woman's reach. The bag had been twisted and crudely pulled tight with a knot.

"Are you all right, my dear?" he asked and immediately felt stupid at having asked such a ridiculous question.

She extended a trembling finger towards the bag.

"You want me to take a look?"

A few moments later, Mr Herman had tapped *999* on his mobile.

"Police, please. Probably an ambulance, too" he told the operator.

Chapter 7

There was already a police presence and an ambulance at Geoffrey Woodman's home when a second patrol car pulled up outside the house and Dixon Clarke scrambled out from the back seat.

He watched as an ambulance crew unloaded a stretcher from their vehicle and entered the house. They left their vehicle's doors wide open which Mabel was quick to spot. She crossed the road and walked slowly past the open doors but not before glancing surreptitiously into the vehicle. Mabel's neighbour across the road raised her tiny binoculars but the ambulance door blocked her view of anything more interesting than the sight of Mabel nonchalantly glancing into the vehicle and scowling. Serves her right! Nosey so-and-so.

*

Dixon was surprised to find that other civilians were already engaged in conversations with

30

police officers.

A man with a small, yapping dog was pointing towards a black, plastic bag to one side of the garden path and a babbling woman was being comforted by a female officer.

"If you're ready, Mr Clarke," said Detective Jack Jackson, pointing at the front door to the house.

Dixon withdrew a key from his pocket and then inserted and turned it in the lock. Once open, he stepped aside and allowed the door to swing slowly open. Detective Jackson stepped into the hallway. He turned towards Dixon and tilted his head as if to ask "*where's the body?*"

"What have you done with the body, sir?"

"*Me?*" What have *I* done with it? Would you like to check my pockets?"

"There's no need for sarcasm, sir."

"Nor stupid questions!" Dixon retorted. "He was right here when I left for the police station," and he pointed towards the area where he had discovered the body surrounded by an irregular pattern of blood-stains on the carpet.

"And you've not been back here since reporting your uncle's murder to us?"

"I have not been back," Dixon muttered.

"Or given the key to somebody else, perhaps?"

"No."

The inspector remained silent for several moments.

"Does anybody else have a key to the house?"

"He has a daughter that lives at the far side of the village. I would imagine she does. I don't know about anyone else."

"Do you have her address?" the inspector enquired as he withdrew a notebook from his jacket pocket.

"Yes, I do. Nine Lupin Lane. It's the turning next to *The Horse and Cart* pub."

Chapter 8

The daughter's name was Josephine Starling, often abbreviated to 'Jo' Starling, and her husband was named Joseph, often abbreviated to 'Joe'. This often led to a degree of misunderstanding and confusion.

Jo was preparing vegetables in the kitchen when the doorbell rang. She put down the potato peeler, wiped her hands on a tea towel and went to answer the door.

Her face registered shock - which rapidly turned to anxiety - as she looked at the faces of a policeman and his female colleague.

"Is Joe all right?" she asked immediately.

"Joe?" the lady asked.

"My husband…"

"We're not here regarding your husband. We understand you have a key to your father's house."

"Well, yes. Why wouldn't I? Is dad okay?"

"We received a visit from one of his neighbours. She called into the station to report suspicious activity at your father's house."

"Suspicious?"

Jo Starling, together with her husband, Joe, were ushered into the back of a waiting police car. The driver revved the engine impatiently and tapped the steering wheel irritably in a short, sharp staccato rhythm. The back door closest to the pair was opened and Jo scrambled across the back seat. She inclined her head towards Joe as he followed her into the car. He took hold of his wife's hand and held it tightly.

"It'll be alright. This has to be a mistake of some kind," but even as he said it he knew how ridiculous it must sound. Ambulances don't cart people off on stretchers for minor scratches or bruises … but then he realised he was allowing his imagination to race faster than the validations of facts.

36

Almost before the car had come to a halt, Jo had grabbed the door handle and shaken off Joe's hold on her arm.

"*Where's my father?*" she blurted out. "Why is there an ambulance? Is he hurt? Is he alright?"

Detective Inspector Jackson stood in front of the door to the house and made it apparent that nobody was going to blunder their way past him until he was good and ready.

"Would you mind confirming exactly who you are, please?"

Joe strode from the car and pushed himself between DI Jackson and his wife.

"She's his daughter, you fool! Let her pass."

37

"And you are …"

"Oh, for Christ's sake! I'm her husband. Tell us what's been going on here … please."

Jackson nudged the door open with his elbow and beckoned Jo into the hallway. Joe pushed past the police inspector and placed his hand on Jo's shoulder.

"Where is he? Can I see him?" Jo asked.

"Who are you expecting to see?" Jackson asked in a half-whisper."

Jo turned to her husband, her face distorted by an anguished expression, unsure how to respond.

"Her father," he half-whispered.

38

The inspector hesitated.

"Is there … a problem?" Joe asked "Is it too awful to …?"

"There is a problem, sir," the officer replied. ***"There is no body!"***

Chapter 9

Mabel could hardly believe what her eyes were telling her! The two ambulance men that had entered the house bearing a stretcher were now leaving the house with the stretcher rolled up under one of their arms! Unless their patient was a jellyfish, why had an ambulance been summoned?

Mabel's neighbour from across the road lowered her small binoculars and placed them on a side table. Later in the day, she would have to bump into Mabel, accidentally, of course, and find out what was happening in that house across the road from her.

*

In fact, there was little, happening in the house across the road. The ambulance had driven away with two disgruntled paramedics sitting up front with the driver.

Detective Inspector Jackson remained inside the house with Jo and Joseph, all three with frowns and puzzled expressions on their faces. The nephew, Dixon Clarke, had sunk into an armchair, tired, perplexed and anxious.

He stared blankly through the living room window at the house opposite. A curtain twitched.

Sycamore Road. Curtains were always twitching but there was rarely the sign of a face.

"Have you an explanation to offer, Mister Clarke, or was this your idea of a sick joke … describing your uncle's mutilated corpse as you did?"

Dixon's features suddenly changed. His cheeks reddened and his eyes flashed wildly.

"You think I made up some cock and bull story? That my imagination ran amok? Perhaps I buried him in the garden! Shall we look to see if the earth has been disturbed?"

"Mr Clarke … these are questions you will be asked whether they come from me or … from someone else."

Dixon sniffed loudly.

"Can you not smell it?" he asked the police inspector.

"The soapy smell? Yes, I noticed it when we entered the room … that and the spotless floor carpet. Not a drop of blood to be seen. Flawless. *Bloodless*. How do you account for that?"

42

"You're supposed to be the detective! You tell me!"

" I wish I could, Mister Clarke. I'm simply repeating what you claim to have seen."

"What I *claim* to have seen? You think I'm making it all up? You think I'm lying?"

"Not at all, sir … but it's all a bit strange, you must admit. No indication of an attack. No body. No sign of any blood."

"This is *not* how the carpet looked when I was here earlier," Dixon remarked.

"You think it did *a runner*?"

"That is quite inappropriate, Inspector."

43

"I agree. I apologise. Forensics should be here shortly. Let's see what they can come up with."

Chapter 10

Mabel really needed to get a little bit of shopping but was torn between the need to find something for her evening meal and keeping an eye on the scene at Mr Woodman's house.

*

The atmosphere inside the house was taut. Jo and Joseph sat beside each other on a settee - Jo staring at the carpet where Dixon claimed to have discovered her father's body and Joseph frowning as he tried to make sense of the scene.

*

"So there's no body, no blood, no sign of a forced entry, his daughter is distraught and neither she nor her husband have anything to offer. The nephew, Dixon Clarke discovered the body, it's face covered in blood … and its tongue cut out, apparently."

"Forensics?" the Chief Inspector asked.

"Nothing. No sign of a forced entry, a disturbance, an attack … nothing."

"Did neighbours see or hear anything unusual?"

"I've got two of my officers knocking on doors but I'm not holding out much hope."

*

The two policewomen had worked their way along the street door by door each taking one side. Eventually, the younger of the two reached Mabel's house. When her doorbell rang and she answered Mabel pretended to look surprised. For the past half hour she had watched as the older police woman had moved from house to house on the opposite side of the street knocking on doors or ringing doorbells.

"Oh dear," she exclaimed. "I hope I haven't done anything wrong. I try so very hard to be a good neighbour. I think it's appreciated, too."

"Not at all, missus …"

46

"Apthorpe. Mabel Apthorpe. Eighteen Catherine Street."

"Er… yes. Thank you. We're making enquiries regarding an incident at the house next to your own."

"That would be Mr Woodman's house then?"

"That's right. You're well-placed to observe any unusual or strange activity, I would imagine."

"I suppose I am," Mabel replied. "Not that I have time to spy on my neighbours, of course."

"Of course."

"Too much housework. There's always such a lot of dust to vacuum up. It's the cars, you see.

There are far too many for a quiet street like ours. It never used to be so bad. Why can't people walk to the shops, that's what I say."

"Yes, well…"

"Anyway, you don't want to hear about my problems, do you? Nobody does, that's the trouble."

The police lady smiled politely.

"Have you noticed anything untoward over the past few days?"

"As I said, I don't have enough hours in the day to be people- watching."

"Right. So you have no information to offer?"

"Now, I didn't say that, did I?"

The police lady smiled again politely.

"He didn't put his dustbin away after it had been emptied and he's usually very strict about that. Just like me. We can't have them blocking the pavement, can we?"

"No, indeed. Have you anything further to add, Mrs Apthorpe?"

"Well… it's nothing really…"

The police officer smiled encouragingly.

"By sheer chance, I happened to see a man go into the house. He parked his Ford Focus outside, unlocked Mr Woodman's front and went in, bold as you like."

"Okay. Did he stay long?"

"That's difficult to say. I don't spend my time staring at strangers, you know. Not like the woman across from me who seems to have plenty of time for staring and gossiping."

As the policewoman made to move away, Mabel suddenly recalled something she'd seen.

"That dustbin I mentioned ... the man with the Ford Focus, when he came back out of the house, he dropped something into that black bin."

Chapter 11

The woman across the road missed nothing as she sneaked another quick glance between the gap in her living-room curtains. The policewoman had spent rather a long time at Mabel's door. She didn't know how fortunate she was to have escaped so easily from Mabel's wagging, lying tongue.

*

The two police ladies stood a little way past Mabel's house and discussed their morning's door-knocking.

"The woman who lives next door to Mr Woodman says Dixon Clarke dropped something into the man's bin as he was leaving."

"Yeah, well, I don't think it could have been a body, do you?"

"She didn't say," her colleague giggled. "He'd have to have had an awfully small body for him to have done that!"

Chapter 12

Josephine Starling did not believe her father had been murdered. He had no enemies, so far as she was aware, and there was nothing of value to steal from the house. Yet …Dixon had reported and described a gruesome scene. The fact was, however, that there was no evidence of a forced entry, no sign of blood on the carpet … and no body!

*

Mabel was awoken from her daydreaming by the rattle of her letterbox followed a few moments later by the near-silent sound of post falling to the floor. *Post*! That was a joke! The only post she got nowadays were demands for bill payments and donation requests to fill charity bags. Other than that, there were numerous leaflets advertising local services and upcoming events in the area. She shuffled to her front door and picked up several small sheets of paper.

'Grass-cutting and garden maintenance services'.

Well, she was perfectly capable of pruning her rose bush without assistance and her small garden had an area of lawn that she could mow in a matter of minutes using the electric mower that she had purchased second-hand from somebody who had placed a postcard in the window of the local post office. The number of times she had almost tripped on the wretched cable didn't bear thinking about.

'One night only! Angus and Sarah McDowell singing traditional Scottish folk songs accompanied by guitar and fiddle.'

Well, she enjoyed a good old sing-along as much as the next person but not in a local pub which is where the couple would be appearing.

Anyway, without bagpipes, how authentic could their performance be? Thank goodness she was too far from the pub to hear any of it. Still, there were a number of folk in her street who, no doubt, would feel quite at home amongst the unruly drinkers exchanging bawdy comments between themselves.

'The Milltown Players proudly present their new production entitled 'The Man with A Runaway Tongue.'

Now that's an interesting title for a play, Mabel thought. *'A runaway tongue'* would be an apt description for the woman across the road. Talk about gossip! She could talk the hind legs off a donkey if she could persuade it to stand still for long enough.

Apart from a charity bag for *The Air Rescue Service* there was nothing more in that day's delivery of items through Mabel's letterbox.

Chapter 13

Dixon Clarke had been questioned by police at some length but they could find nothing that might link him to the death or disappearance of Geoffrey Woodman.

Josephine Starling was no longer distraught but she was quite angry. She did not believe for one moment that any harm had come to her father but it was unlike him not to let her know if he intended to be away for more than a couple of days. The body, though. That terrified her. What could Dixon Clarke possibly have seen? He'd seen a body …but there was no body. He'd seen blood on the carpet…but there were no bloodstains. The room had been as neat and tidy as her father always kept it. What on earth was going on?

*

The woman across the road was curious. She wasn't a nosey woman but at the back of her mind something nagged away at her composure.

When the man with the Ford Focus had come out of Mr Woodman's house he had dropped a

57

black bag in the dustbin. In the present circumstances, she felt entitled to be curious. She had a thought but before she could act upon it the day needed to have grown dark. She would wait until nightfall.

*

Somewhat incredibly, the police had decided that it was too soon to describe Geoffrey Woodman as '*a missing person*'. Barely forty-eight hours had passed since Dixon Clarke had found the blood-stained body with its mangled face.

Nevertheless…Mabel just knew that the man driving the blue Ford Focus had been up to no good and she was determined to see what was in that black bag.

Chapter 14

The woman across the road felt it was time to draw the curtains in her front room. If she turned on a light without closing them, anybody passing would see her clearly silhouetted through the bay window. She pressed the button on her reclining armchair and lowered its legs. Crossing the floor to the window, she thought she saw a movement by Mabel Apthorpe's front door.

She was right!

Mabel was standing on her doorstep and looking

both ways, up and down the street.

The woman across the road edged back behind the curtains and peeked through the narrow slit between them.

Mabel stepped cautiously towards her front garden gate leaving her front door ajar. As she opened the gate, Mabel again checked that she was alone and unseen. Or *thought* she was!

*

Mabel felt certain she was alone and unseen as she opened the gate and stepped hesitantly on to the pavement. She knew Mr Woodman's black bin hadn't been moved into his back yard because she would have heard his gate squeaking as he opened it.

She felt safe from sight as she took the few steps needed to reach the bin. Other than the glow of a street lamp twenty yards away, she would be hidden from sight by darkness. The gardening gloves she had taken from her shed would leave no fingerprints. Mabel had watched sufficient television dramas to know how thieves and crooks went about their business … not that she was either, of course!

*

The woman from across the road was enjoying the best treat she had known for a very long time. She watched as Mabel lifted the dustbin

lid, leaned in, and pulled out a black plastic bag.
Now what, she wondered? She polished the lens
on her tiny binoculars.

*

Mabel took another look about her and silently
lowered the dustbin's lid. Still clutching the
black bag, she returned to her home and quietly
shut its front door. Going from her living room
through to her kitchen, she took off the
gardening gloves and slid open a cutlery drawer.
Having withdrawn a pair of scissors, she
carefully cut along the top edge of the black bag.
Ridiculous though it was, she looked over her
shoulder to reassure herself she was unobserved
… and then thrust her right hand into the bag.

Chapter 15

Occasionally, the woman who lived across the road would visit the local cinema. Her tastes were quite limited. A good thriller suited her best. She reckoned that what she had just witnessed had the makings of such a film. Her near-neighbour across the road, Mabel, had actually come out of her house, gone to Mr Woodman's black dustbin, opened its lid, pulled out a bag of some kind and then returned home with it. *It defied understanding!* Then a thought struck her. Could Mabel Apthorpe be in any way connected to Mr Woodman's mysterious disappearance?

*

The woman from across the road was having a restless night.

What should she do? Report Mabel's odd behaviour to the police? They'd laugh at her. Confront Mabel? If Mabel had harmed Mr Woodman what was to prevent her doing the same to another neighbour - namely, her!

"I know," she thought to herself, "I'll mention it ever-so-discretely to Brenda in the grocery shop tomorrow morning."

Chapter 16

The police didn't know what to think but as there was no sign of a mutilated body and no indication of a crime, vicious or otherwise, having taken place, they were content to let matters rest for the immediate time being.

*

Mabel placed her right hand into the plastic bag and screamed. Her fingers had touched something soft and slimy. What could the man with the blue Ford Focus have dumped in the bag? She let out a smothered scream … a dead mouse? She was afraid of mice and most creepy-crawlies. Some discarded vegetables, perhaps?

She sniffed tentatively but couldn't detect the characteristic smell of rotting greens.

Mabel laid a sheet of the previous day's local newspaper on her kitchen table. She closed her eyes, for no reason she could explain through logic, and tipped the contents of the bag onto the paper.

*

The sound of an ambulance siren close by startled those out strolling in the evening's mild air. Jo and her husband could hear it as they sat in their back garden sipping a favourite white wine.

"I wonder who it is," Jo said. "Do you think

they've found my dad?"

"There's no point thinking like that!" Joe retorted.

"I know but every time I hear that wailing sound I can't help feeling that something really awful has happened to my dad."

"The police said they would contact you if there was any new information regarding his disappearance."

"No news is bad news. It has to be." Jo clasped her husband's hand and sobbed.

67

Chapter 17

Mabel screamed. She couldn't help herself.

She'd tipped the contents of the black plastic bag onto her kitchen table and something damp and slimy had slithered out.

*

The woman across the road heard the scream. At least, it sounded like a scream. It was difficult to tell at such a distance. She shrugged her shoulders. It was probably no more than a shriek of laughter. She thought Mabel was fortunate to have something to laugh about. What with high prices, aches and pains and a bad back there was little enough to amuse her these days.

*

Mr Woodman woke up in a hospital bed. How long had he been here? Why was he there? The light in his room was bright but it was dark beyond the large windows. His head was aching and one of his arms had been bandaged. He tried to recall the events that had brought him here but they were still somewhat hazy. He frowned. There had been a lot of shouting, a scuffle and a glint of light from the blade of a knife.

*

Mabel Apthorpe prodded the sloppy item with a fork and decided that her scream had been something of an overreaction. Whatever it was, it wasn't human!

There was a small piece of the original wrapper stuck to it and a little more prodding revealed the words '*Halloumi (contains goat's and sheep's milk)*.

Halloumi? What on earth was halloumi? Another of those strange foreign foods that filled the supermarket shelves these days! Well, she certainly didn't intend using **halloumi** as a sandwich filling any time soon! In any case, it had been thrown into the dustbin so it was probably mouldy.

Mabel sniffed the halloumi, found the smell repugnant, wrapped it in the sheet of newspaper, and tossed it into her blue dustbin.

Chapter 18

Veronica Williams played the part of a British spy in The Milltown Players production of '*The Man with A Runaway Tongue.*' Since Geoffrey Woodman's unfortunate accident, she had been forced to rehearse alongside a new co-star. He had learnt his lines, was confident on stage, but lacked the chemistry that had existed between Geoffrey and herself. Rehearsals took up less time now the play had gone 'live' and she resolved to catch a bus from the park-and-ride and visit him later that morning.

*

Billy Brown was affectionately known among the theatre's staff as *The Broomstick*. He was responsible for clearing and cleaning the stage after each performance by The Milltown Players. He could never be sure what he'd find but that was half the pleasure. The other half was a free ticket to each performance.

*

Geoffrey Woodman groaned but not as loudly as he had a couple of days ago. The accident on stage had been careless of him particularly as he had even gone to the lengths of practising his stage moves at home in the living room. He smiled to himself. *By God, he was good!* He'd even fooled his sharp-witted son-in-law!

His role in the play would pass to the young understudy, Christopher Thompson, who was new to the drama group but a quick learner.

"What I must do," Geoffrey Woodman thought, "is to try contacting Jo to let her know where I am. She'll be thinking something terrible has happened to me!"

Chapter 19

The woman across the road was well-respected within her immediate community. She knew this without the need for confirmation. Each summer, she attended the Women's Institute local fete even though there were some quite outspoken and self-opinionated members.

Although not a member herself (she was far too busy minding her own business to be involved in theirs) she felt she was representing Sycamore Road. Somebody had to and Mabel Apthorpe certainly showed no interest in doing so … and she always purchased a ticket for the lucky dip so she felt wholly vindicated.

The woman from across the road wondered why Mabel had rooted around in Mr Woodman's dustbin. She'd pulled a bag from out of it and carried it into her own house. What could she want with a dirty old bag? Not that she cared. It was none of her business.

*

Geoffrey Woodman waited until the nurse had finished speaking to a member of staff and then called out.

"Excuse me," he said. "Am I able to contact my daughter, please?"

"Do you not have a mobile?"

"Er… no. I usually rely on my landline."

The nurse looked surprised but walked away and returned a couple of minutes later with a bedside console and a traditional black plug-in telephone.

Geoffrey was not good at remembering

numbers, particularly mobile numbers, but at the third attempt he was relieved to hear his daughter's voice.

"Jo speaking."

"Jo, it's me … dad. I had a little accident."

There was a stunned silence.

"Dad? Is that really you?"

"Yes, of course, don't sound so surprised."

"But I … we … thought you must be…"

"Must be what? Look, I can't stay on this phone for long but don't worry. I hurt my head when I tripped on a stage prop but I'm going to be fine and should be home in a day or two.

*

Billy Brown, *The Broomstick*, swept the stage and began to tidy away the props that needed storing ready for the next night's performance.

Geoffrey Woodman had been his usual disorganised self and left his sinister blood-splattered sheet centre stage on the floor. Had he been a little tidier he would have put it away in his locker and it wouldn't have been there for him to trip over and cause him to end up in hospital! Billy looked at the messy red stains on the ragged, torn bed-sheet and tut-tutted. If the

77

blood had been real he'd have had a job cleaning the stage!

Chapter 20

"What was he thinking of? Why didn't he phone me and explain what had happened?"

Joseph sighed.

"Come on, Jo, the poor man was probably concussed. It sounds like he took quite a hit when he tripped and smacked his head on the stage floor."

"Okay. I'll go along with that but have you forgotten how Dixon described finding him in a

pool of blood with his throat cut and minus a
tongue?"

"Okay. Sorry. You win. I'm just not thinking
straight."

"I'm sure there has to be a simple explanation
for all of this," Joseph suggested.

"Are you? Are you really sure" Jo asked.

"No," Joseph replied.

*

When Dixon contacted Jo on his landline he was
relieved when she answered within five seconds.

"I wondered if you had any news about …" he

began.

"Dad's in hospital. He took a tumble on stage and they're keeping an eye on him."

Dixon fell silent for several moments.

"He's not …?"

"He's not dead if that's what you're asking," Jo said.

"But I … look I'm sorry to say this but … the body … the blood…"

"And I'm sorry to say this but you've caused us all unnecessary distress. How could you?"

"I know what I saw," Dixon insisted. "I went to

the police and explained what had happened …
not that I knew, I could only report what I saw."

"But there was nothing to see!" Jo was
practically shouting down the phone. "How
could you?"

Dixon fell silent.

"Are you still there?" Jo asked. "Look, I'm
sorry. I shouldn't have shouted at you like that."

"It's understandable," Dexter said quietly.
"Anyway, give me the name of the hospital and
I'll call in and try to make some sense of it all."

*

To reach the hospital, Dexter had to pass quite

close to Sycamore Close. He decided to go to Geoffrey's house, not simply to enter the living room and scratch his head again, but to seek out a small suitcase, gather together clothing, a shaver and washing materials and take it to the hospital for his uncle.

His brow was still furrowed ten minutes later when he let himself out and locked the door behind him.

*

Mabel had heard the blue Ford Focus draw up outside Mr Woodman's home and by surreptitiously squinting from the side of a curtain confirmed that it was the same man that had arrived the other day when the police were in attendance.

Looking at her watch as the man left, not one of those fashionable so-called 'smart' watches that had no dial or minute hand, she ascertained that he had been in Mr Woodman's house for no more than ten minutes. Plenty of time to remove any incriminating evidence, she thought.

*

The woman across the road immediately recognised the blue car that had pulled up on the opposite side of the road. She also recognised Mabel's nose and grey, curly hair poking through the curtains. That woman never misses a thing, she thought. Nosey woman! After ten minutes, the man left the house and the woman across the road wished she still had her old Kodak camera. The police would have praised her for snapping a villain and the local newspaper would have run a story about her … not that she actually sought publicity for being so public-spirited.

Chapter 21

Dexter discovered his uncle on *Level 2* of the hospital with his head propped up by a pillow,

"Hello, Uncle. I'm pleased to see you looking so well. You look remarkably healthy for someone who had their throat cut and their tongue sliced off!"

Geoffrey Woodman forced a smile and said apologetically,

"I made it appear so realistic, did I not? I certainly had you fooled."

Dexter was in two minds whether to laugh out loud or strangle the man where he lay.

"You were surrounded by a pool of blood!"

"Very realistic, eh? I borrowed the spare blood sheet from the theatre props cupboard."

"What the devil is a ***blood sheet***?" Dexter spluttered.

"It's something I designed myself for use in our production of '*The Man with A Runaway Tongue*'. The play's about a British agent who trades secrets in return for money and a safe haven. I simply took an old bed sheet into my backyard and sprayed it with splotches of a reddish paint."

"Leaving your carpet spotless, of course," Dexter mused.

After a moment or two's thought, he frowned and asked another question.

"You lay with your mouth open. You did that

deliberately, didn't you?"

"Yes, I'm afraid so. It wasn't that easy but I'd curled my tongue into the roof of my mouth and slid it partly down my throat."

"That must have been unpleasant," Dexter remarked.

"It was but you only took a brief look. I was able to roll it back down soon after I'd fooled you into believing it was lying beside my head."

"What I actually saw was a chunk of halloumi rolled into the shape of a tongue! *Correct*?"

"Indeed …but you were fooled at first?"

"I suppose so. It stank so I slung it in a black bag

from your kitchen drawer and dumped it in your black bin."

"That was a mistake."

"A *mistake*? Why was it a mistake?"

"It should have been the green bin."

The two men, one elderly, the other young, regarded each other for several moments before Dexter shrugged his shoulders and pointed at the small suitcase.

"Any way, I've brought some stuff in for you … clothes and wash things although they're thinking of chucking you out tomorrow."

"Thank you. That's thoughtful. My back lawn

will need mowing as soon as I get back or Mabel will start to think I really *have* been murdered and won't be returning to my flock of adoring neighbours."

Chapter 22

The woman across the road was lost in her own thoughts. Mabel had definitely been acting strangely and the police had come calling, hadn't they? They seemed to spend far longer at Mabel's house than at any other. There had to be a reason for that. The most likely reason would be that Mabel was trying to divert suspicion away from herself and to direct it at *me*! Well, we'd soon see about that.

*

Yet again, the blue Ford Focus pulled to a halt outside Mr Woodman's house. This time, two men got out of the car. A day had passed and Dexter had collected his uncle from the hospital.

Mabel had just opened her front door to fetch a milk bottle from its doorstep. She saw the two men and her head whirled.

Mr Woodman was home! Nothing dreadful had happened to him although he appeared to be limping slightly but then who didn't when they grew old.

*

"Hello, Mabel," Mr Woodman called out.

90

"Everything okay? No break ins, no burglars, no fires?"

"Everything's fine, Mr Woodman. I hope you won't be cross with me but I took the liberty of removing a bag from your black bin. It was whiffing a bit and so I took it out and wrapped it in newspaper and put it in the *blue* bin!"

"The *blue* bin?" Mr Woodman raised his eyebrows. "I got it wrong again, didn't I? I can never remember what goes where!"

"The woman across the road saw me rummaging in your bin so don't be surprised if she comes over and informs on me!"

Mr Woodman glanced over his shoulder and

caught the woman at her window standing and staring across at them.

"Did the new play go down well?" Mabel thought to ask. "I had a leaflet through the door."

"Oh, I think so," Mr Woodman replied before adding in a jocular voice, "although I think I scored more of a hit *after* the play when I tripped and fell!"

*

The woman across the road now knew for certain that she was being talked about. She'd seen both Mabel and Mr Woodman turn and stare at her with accusing eyes. As if she had anything to feel guilty about … a kind and considerate resident in a street that was rapidly going downhill. Brats racing around on those wretched scooters and not only on the road. On the pavement, too! Dustbins left out after their collection day. Neighbours like Mabel gossiping and spreading lies about her.

How much more could she take before she lost her mind and was despatched to the loony bin?

Chapter 23

There was hardly a star to be seen in the night sky and even the moon was hidden behind thick

93

clouds. The street lamp, surprise, surprise, was out of order again but there were fresh batteries in her torch. She crossed the road silently in her slippers and stood outside Mabel's house. There was nobody on the street, not even that man who started up his motorbike late at night to go off to work as a security guard somewhere or other. She rang the doorbell.

*

Mabel jumped when she heard her doorbell sound. Who could possibly be at her door at this time of night? Her only regular caller was the lady from Social Services who kept an eye on her and made sure she was eating and drinking enough water.

Never after four in the afternoon, though.

Perhaps Mr Woodman had stumbled on his bad leg and hurt himself … but he probably had one of those clever, no, *smart* phones, so he would have called his daughter or the man who owned the blue Ford Focus.

A burglar then? Did burglars ring doorbells? She thought not. Her front room curtains were drawn and, in any case, it was far too dark to see who was at her door.

Mabel removed the chain on the inside of her front door, drew back the bolt and opened it a chink.

"It's only me, Mabel," said the woman from

across the road.

After a few moments of hesitation, Mabel called out, "what is it you want? It's very late, you know and I was about to go to bed."

"I only wanted a quick word with you and it's quite urgent."

It's surely not a matter of life or death, Mabel thought.

She opened the door another couple of inches.

"Please let me in," said the woman from across the road. "I won't keep you more than a minute or two and then you can enjoy a good, long sleep."

Mabel sighed deeply. She knew very little about her neighbour across the road even though she was only a small stone's throw away … but the woman must be desperate to come calling at this time of night.

Mabel opened the door fully and the woman stepped into the hallway.

"How can I help you?" Mabel asked politely.

"Well, for a start, you can stop spreading gossip about me!"

Mabel was dumbstruck.

"Gossip? What gossip? I never gossip about my friends and neighbours."

"I've seen you talking about me to Mr Woodman. Don't think I haven't been watching you both."

"We do *not* gossip and we certainly haven't mentioned you in any of our conversations."

"*Really?* Pull the other one, it's got bells on."

"I've no idea what you're talking about," Mabel said and began to feel slightly anxious.

"I honestly don't know what you mean," she said.

"*Honesty*? When did that word ever enter your vocabulary?"

Mabel's anxiety grew … which is when she

noticed the Tesco carrier bag her neighbour was carrying.

"What's in your bag?" she asked uneasily.

"Oh, you'll find out soon enough!"

*

The woman from across the road raised her arm and pushed Mabel further into the hallway and then, with her other arm, swung the Tesco bag towards Mabel's head, forcing her to back into the living room.

"*Mr Woodman*!" she screamed.

"Your partner in lie-spreading won't hear you, my dear. He's busy delivering his lines again at the theatre."

"And you …what…?

"*I'm* delivering justice … no postage to pay … no signature required …I'm delivering it free and in person …here in your cosy spy-nest."

"Look … why don't I put the kettle on and we can chat over cups of tea?"

"*Cups of tea*?" The woman from across the road spat contemptuously. "You really think *a cup of tea* will wash away all the bitterness and hatred you have spread about me all these years?"

"I've done no such thing!" Mabel retorted as she edged back towards the door.

"Anyway, *I* could do with a drink. I'll fill the kettle."

As she turned to head for the kitchen, Mabel heard a swishing sound and spun around just in time to see the hammer bearing down on her head.

Chapter 24

Veronica Williams was all smiles as she welcomed Geoffrey back into his role as the garrulous spy.

"*The Man with A Runaway Tongue* has finally returned with a limping leg," he said.

Veronica offered a sympathetic smile.

"We could cast you as Long John Silver, perhaps."

She noted the steely look that entered his eyes and added, "Christopher will be disappointed, of course. He was quite enjoying his first serious role with us."

"I can understand his frustration but he's still young and there's plenty of time for him to demonstrate his ability and to take advantage of the countless opportunities that will, no doubt, come his way."

"So it's back to the blood and gore again in ten minutes. Billy Brown has the spare sheet of blood ready for you."

"Ah, well, I won't need it. As you see, I've brought the original with me," Geoffrey replied and pulled the hideous sheet from his backpack.

"I've brought along another tongue, too!" he added. "My neighbour found the original in my black bin and mistook it for a slice of halloumi."

"Really? Why would she think that?"

"I'd rolled it up in an old halloumi wrapper before tossing it in the bin. These dummy tongues are single-use only."

Veronica laughed.

"You're a true professional."

Chapter 25

Mabel moaned. She tried to move onto her knees but fell back into the black mist that enveloped her.

"You're not saying much now, are you, my dear?" The woman from across the road laughed hysterically. "Sadly for you, you'll be in no state to continue spreading your foul accusations against me."

"I haven't …" but Mabel was too dazed to say more. Her head was throbbing, spinning … *oh, God, but it hurt!*

"Does it hurt?" The woman laughed. "Don't worry, my dear. In a few moments you won't feel any pain at all."

The next hammer blow rendered Mabel unconscious.

It was as well she was unconscious because what happened next would have stopped her heart dead.

Chapter 26

"You know what we do with our country's spies if they trade secrets to our enemies?" the spymaster asked tersely.

"Something unpleasant, I dare say," the traitor answered.

"Unpleasant is not the word I would choose, old boy. Your runaway tongue has run away with any words you might have voiced in future."

The man accused of betraying his country was silent for several moments.

"Will I die?"

"Will you die?"

His interrogator gave a short laugh.

"Eventually ... "

He put a knife to the traitor's throat and, as he

briefly turned his back on the audience, pulled a thin sheet speckled with red paint from inside his jumper and placed it beneath the traitor's head and shoulders. It was a tense moment for the actor. Sometimes it didn't go quite so smoothly!

He half-turned towards the stunned audience before swinging back his arm and driving the knife's blade into the traitor's neck.

Several members of the audience screamed but their screams were not as loud as that emitted by the traitor as his torturer forced open his mouth and hacked out his tongue.

The audience gasped as he tossed it into the air and watched it land with a dull thump several feet away.

"Sorry, chum. *Just doing my job*."

The actor always felt a moment of panic at this point. Suppose some crazy member of staff was to swap the retractable-bladed knife for a real one!

*

The play concluded and the audience applauded enthusiastically as they headed for the nearest exit leaving the cast to clear up and return home.

"I thought it went well tonight," Veronica remarked, "and no horrible accidents!"

"No extra work for *The Broomstick* either. I've tidied up and put all my fake blood and gore into the cupboard."

Veronica pecked his cheek.

"A true professional, my dear, as ever."

Chapter 27

The woman from across the road hadn't quite finished with that tell-tale neighbour of hers. The blabbermouth wouldn't be spreading lies and rumours about her for quite some time. She wiped the blood from the meat knife on Mabel's dress and put it back into the bag she had brought together with the hammer.

She opened the front door of Mabel's house quietly, leaving it slightly ajar. She didn't want to disturb the sleep or television-viewing of her neighbours. She was considerate like that. Before crossing the road, she went to the house next door to Mabel's and pushed a handwritten note through its letterbox.

Chapter 28

Geoffrey Woodman sighed as he finally reached his home. The pressure of remembering his lines, his character in the play and the costume changes between scenes, always left him exhausted. Fortunately, it was a mild evening and he quite welcomed the twenty minute walk back home.

It was a dark night but he noticed a piece of

paper sticking out from his letterbox. Frowning, he tugged it free, turned the key in its lock and entered his home. He could have gone straight to bed, he felt that exhausted, but boiled water in a kettle for a cup of tea. Then he read the note.

*

'You should visit your next door neighbour before it's too late. If she still had a tongue, she'd have some story to tell you! For once, the gossipmonger would be telling the truth about me instead of all those made-up lies. Don't come looking for me because you won't find me ~ unless you enjoy a midnight swim in the river! I won't be punished for what I have done and my conscience is clear. No doubt, the gossip will

continue to flow, with or without Mabel and her sort, but it will no longer trouble me. Revenge is not sweet but it brings about a satisfaction and a calmness that will allow me to R.I.P.

From the woman across the road.'

terry@terrybraverman.co.uk

amazon/books/terence braverman

updates: www.noteablemusic.co.uk

AVAILABLE BOOKS

(July 2023)

**WHISKERS, WINGS and BUSHY TAILS
book series (Stories from Undermead):**

The Inner Mystic Circle

The Race

Curly Cat

Dotty Dormouse

Blackberry Pie

113

George and the Magic Jigsaw

Rain! Rain! Rain!

Where is Dotty Dormouse?

Tap! Tap! Tap!

SwaggerWagger

Three Wheels and a Bell

The Chase

Blackberry Bluff

Rebellion

Autumn

Quiz Night

Black as Night

*****

115

Millie Manx (The Tale of a Tail)

Granddad Remembers (But is he telling the truth?)

Ninky and Nurdle (Stories from Noodle-Land)

The Playground of Dreams

What Can I Do When It's Raining Outside?

Buggy Babes

More...

CRIME

Time to Kill

Stage Fright

ROMANCE

The Man from Blue Anchor

A TWIST IN THE TALE

(Open Pandora's Box and what will you find?)
25 stories with 'a twist in the tale':

A Night at the Castle

Baby Jane

The Christmas Fairy

Pressure

Baby

The Little Bedroom

Bulls Eye

The Missing Money

The Retirement Party

The Tartan Scarf

A Case of Mistaken Identity

The Doughnut Man

Mister Myson

July 2023

119

Printed in Great Britain
by Amazon

24186992R00069